The ★ Capitol

A Meet the Nation's Capitol Book

For Bucko,
who didn't get to see this book finished
but loved to tell stories from history. You'll forever
be on the pages of this book, among the paintings,
because I know you would have loved that.
Just look for the red suspenders.
Love always,

Lindsay

Special Thanks

I would like to share my deep gratitude to the following people who helped
me create this book. Without them it would not be possible. It truly takes a village.
Clelia Gore, Clarissa Wong, Erica De Chavez, Frank Tupta, Theresa and Stephen
White, Brandon Naylor, Jane Campbell, Ronn Jackson, all the expert readers, and
the folks at the United States Historical Society and Architect of the Capitol.
Thank you, thank you!

The Capitol: A Meet the Nation's Capitol Book
Copyright © 2022 by Lindsay Ward
All rights reserved. Manufactured in Italy.
No part of this book may be used or reproduced in any manner whatsoever without written
permission except in the case of brief quotations embodied in critical articles and reviews. For information address
HarperCollins Children's Books, a division of HarperCollins Publishers, 195 Broadway, New York, NY 10007.
www.harpercollinschildrens.com

Library of Congress Control Number: 2021943543
ISBN 978-0-06-320380-8

The artist used and did the following in order to complete this book: an iPad Pro, lots and lots of coffee, audiobooks,
political thriller movies, Sylvan Esso on repeat, and working in various locations, including a hair salon. Oh, and magic.
Because there is no other way to explain how all these digital illustrations got done in less than two months.
Typography by Erica De Chavez   22 23 24 25 26   RTLO   10 9 8 7 6 5 4 3 2 1   ❖   First Edition

The ★ Capitol

A Meet the Nation's Capitol Book

Lindsay Ward

HARPER

An Imprint of HarperCollinsPublishers

WELCOME TO THE UNITED STATES CAPITOL!

The Capitol is the meeting place of the **United States Congress**: the **Senate** and **House of Representatives**, which compose the **legislative branch**.

There are three branches of the United States government: legislative, executive, and judicial.

The Capitol is both a national **monument** and a working office. Millions of people visit the Capitol every year.

DID YOU KNOW?

Congress first met in the Capitol Building on November 17, 1800.

Have you ever been to the Capitol?

Let's look at the people who work there.
What do they do?

Administration

Payroll Officer · Budget Officer · Accountant · Lawyer

Cleaning Crew

Janitor · Custodial Supervisor · Recycler

Capitol Police

Chief of Police · Police Officer

Capitol Guide Service

Professional Tour Guides

Medical Staff

Doctor · Nurse

Food Services

Chef · Dishwasher · Server · Host

Gift Shop

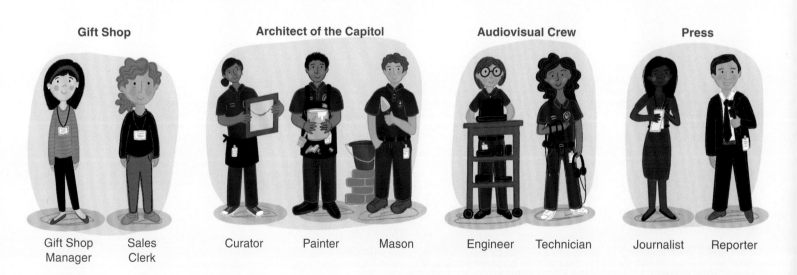

Gift Shop Manager · Sales Clerk

Architect of the Capitol

Curator · Painter · Mason

Audiovisual Crew

Engineer · Technician

Press

Journalist · Reporter

Wow! That's a lot of people! Can you count them all?
There are many different types of jobs in the Capitol.

Some people who work in the Capitol help make laws and represent the voices of the people. Some give tours to visitors and teach them about United States history. Others protect and take care of the building itself.

SENATE

Constitutionally Mandated Officers

Vice President of the United States | President pro Tempore | Reading Clerk | Clerk of the Senate

Senators

Majority Leader | Minority Leader | Whips

Senate-elected Officers and Officials

Secretary of Senate | Sergeant at Arms | Senate Parliamentarian | Secretary for the Majority | Secretary for the Minority | Senate Chaplain

Appointed Senate Officers

Senate Historian | Senate Curator

HOUSE OF REPRESENTATIVES

Representatives

Speaker of the House | Assistant Speaker | Majority Leader | Minority Leader | Whips

House-elected Officers and Officials

Chief Administrative Officer | Clerk of the House | Sergeant at Arms | Chaplain of the House

Appointed House Officers

General Counsel | Legislative Counsel | House Parliamentarian | House Historian | Inspector General | House Curator

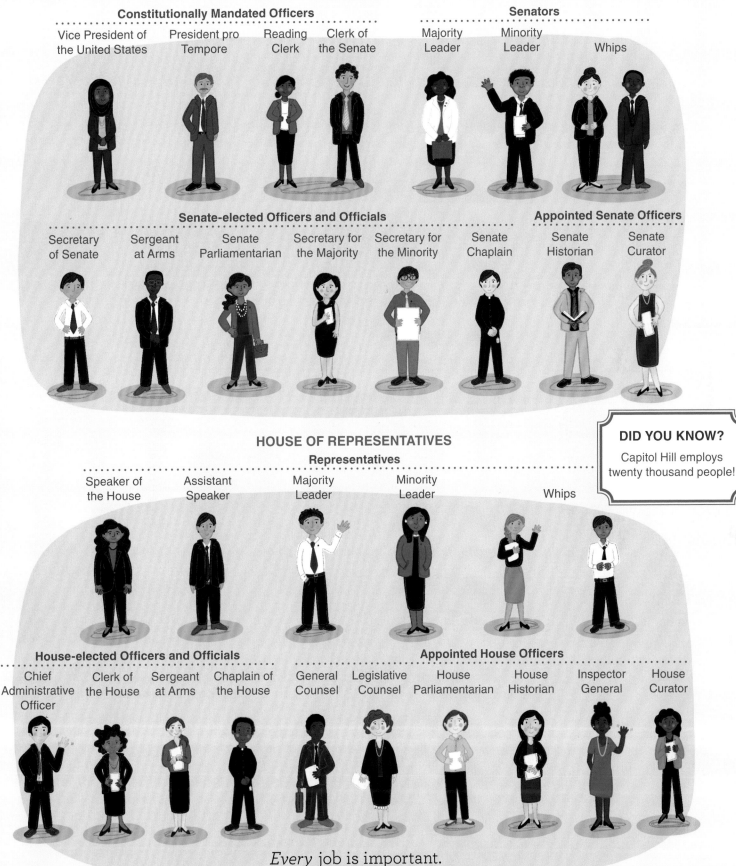

DID YOU KNOW?
Capitol Hill employs twenty thousand people!

Every job is important.

Lots of people are visiting the Capitol today.

This is Peter. He is visiting his dad, a **mason** at the Capitol.

Nima is here to meet her mom. Nima's mom is a United States **senator**.

Can you find the Statue of Freedom?

DID YOU KNOW?

In the center of Emancipation Hall sits Thomas Crawford's model for the Statue of Freedom. In 1860, casting for the Statue of Freedom began. It was to sit on the dome of the Capitol. Philip Reid, an enslaved worker at the foundry, engineered a way to disassemble the sections using a pulley-and-tackle system. By the time the Statue of Freedom was ready to be installed atop the dome in December 1863, Philip Reid was a free man.

Gabriel is helping his grandma. She is a member of the Capitol Guide Service, which gives tours to visitors. Gabriel hands out headphones as he and his grandma greet visitors arriving at the Capitol.

The Capitol is a huge place! It has five floors. With the connecting Capitol Visitor Center, it covers over 1.5 million square feet.

Wow, that's big! Can you guess which sections Peter, Nima, and Gabriel will visit today?

HOUSE CHAMBER

SOUTH WING

COX CORRIDORS

NATIONAL STATUARY HALL

DID YOU KNOW?

Building began for the United States Capitol in 1793, in a time without power tools or any modern machinery.

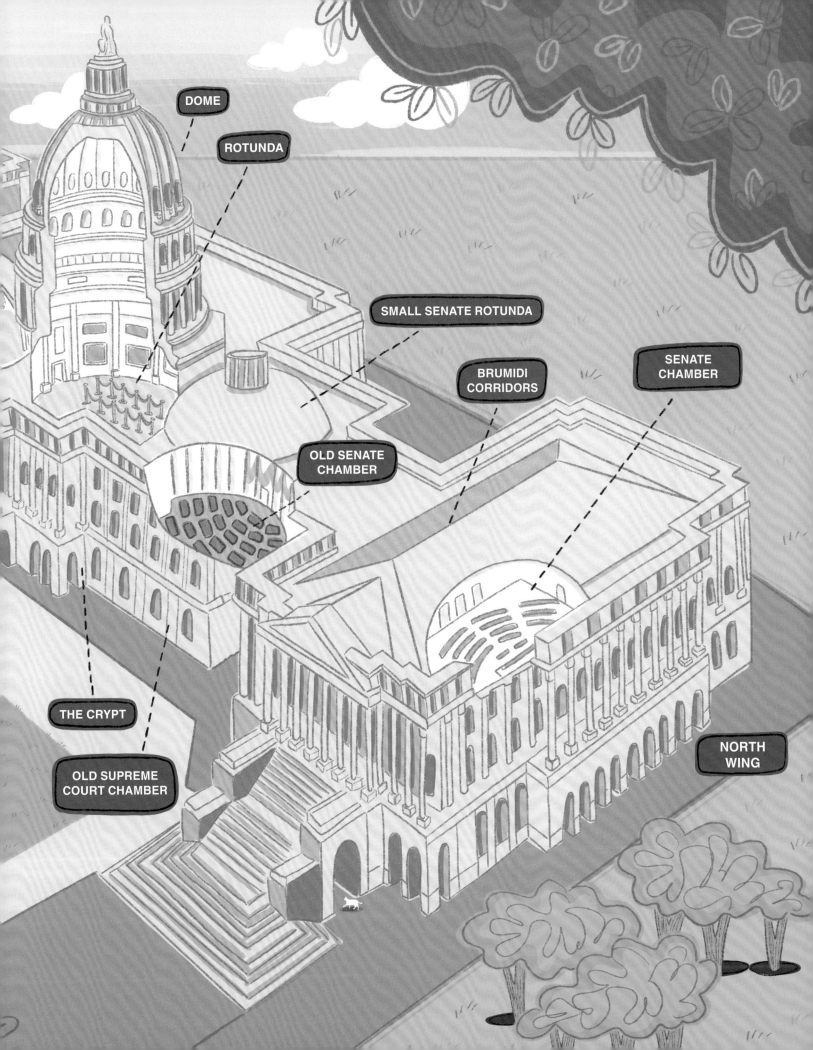

Peter walks to the **Senate Wing** with his dad. They pass through the Crypt and head toward the Small Senate Rotunda.

Can you find the compass stone on the floor in the Crypt?

DID YOU KNOW?
The compass stone in the floor of the Crypt represents where the four quadrants of Washington, DC, come together.

Today, Peter's dad is pouring concrete to repair a section of the floor in the Capitol. Peter's dad is one of many skilled workers who make up the office of the Architect of the Capitol.

The Architect of the Capitol takes care of all the buildings on Capitol Hill, including the Capitol. They employ more than two thousand people. Meet the members of the Architect of the Capitol:

ARCHITECT

Preserves and maintains the architectural integrity of the Capitol.

ELECTRICIAN

Maintains, preserves, and refurbishes thousands of miles of electrical wiring and over 100,000 light fixtures.

ENGINEER

Maintains electrical, mechanical, civil, safety, plumbing, and environmental structures throughout the Capitol.

SUBWAY OPERATOR

Drives and operates the subway system below the Capitol.

PLUMBER

Maintains, repairs, and cares for all plumbing and piping systems in the Capitol.

TOUR GUIDE

Meets, greets, and guides visitors through the Capitol.

MECHANIC

Maintains and repairs all mechanical and digital equipment in the Capitol.

PHOTOGRAPHER

Captures events, artifacts, and seasons at the Capitol.

Each worker has a unique skill set.
Together, they make sure the Capitol and
grounds are preserved and maintained.

PRESERVATIONIST

Preserves and maintains historical
objects, monuments, and furniture
throughout the Capitol.

PAINTER

Maintains and cares for all
ornamental painting in the Capitol.

ARCHIVIST

Researches, preserves, and
maintains historical documents in
the Architect of the Capitol archives.

GARDENER

Takes care of all the gardens
and landscapes on the 58 acres
surrounding the Capitol.

WOODWORKER

Uses old and modern techniques to
preserve and maintain woodwork, cabinetry,
and doors throughout the Capitol.

PLASTERER

Maintains and preserves
plaster throughout the Capitol.

CURATOR

Conserves and maintains art,
artifacts, buildings, rooms, and
landscapes around the Capitol.

MASON

Preserves and cares for
all the stone, marble, brick,
and granite in the Capitol.

Do you know anyone who does a job like these?

What are those? Peter stops just before the wet concrete his dad has poured in front of the Old Supreme Court Chamber.

DID YOU KNOW?
The Old Supreme Court Chamber was used as the courtroom of the Supreme Court from 1810 to 1860.

Peter's dad radios to the **Capitol Police**
and explains the situation.

There's a cat loose in the Capitol.

We are on it. Thanks, James!

The Capitol has its own police force. The Capitol Police are in charge of safeguarding and patrolling the United States Capitol Complex.

Peter and his dad look around. They walk through the Senate Connecting Corridor, down the **Brumidi Corridors**, and up the East Grand Staircase.

Hmmm . . .

No cat!

DID YOU KNOW?

The artist Constantino Brumidi based the elaborate decorative scheme in the Brumidi Corridors on Raphael's Loggia from the Vatican in Rome. Brumidi painted most of the murals between 1857 and 1859, when the Senate moved into the wing.

Then Peter sees a flicker of white
heading up the stairs to the **Senate Gallery**.

Peter and his dad rush up the stairs . . .

... and find Nima sitting in the gallery, but *not* the cat. Nima is on the soccer team with Peter. Nima is waiting for her mom while the Senate is in session.

Do you see the cat? What is it doing?

Inside the **Senate Chamber**, a hundred United States senators, two from each state, represent the voices of their citizens while discussing, debating, and voting on policy and legislation.

Nima tells her mom's **chief of staff**, Thomas, that she'll meet her mom later.

There's a whole team of people who help each senator and representative do their job. These are the people who help them:

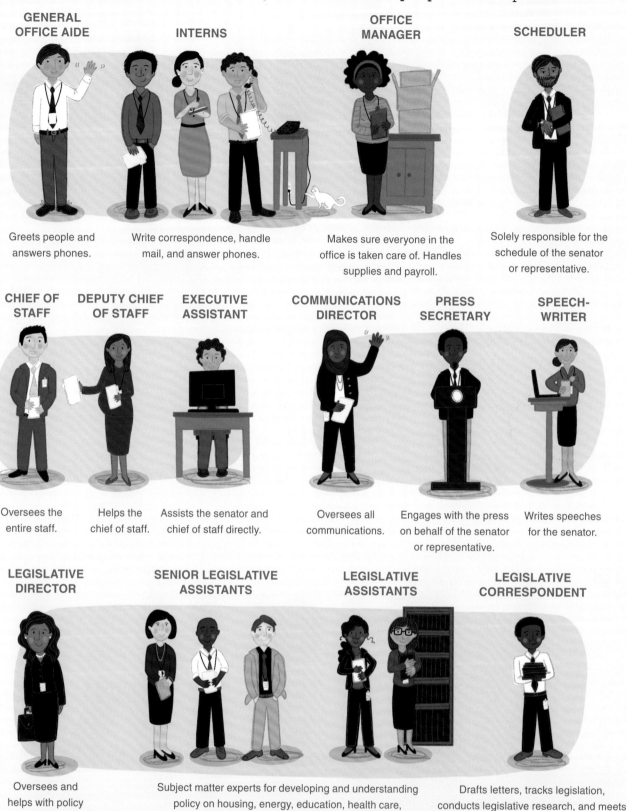

GENERAL OFFICE AIDE
Greets people and answers phones.

INTERNS
Write correspondence, handle mail, and answer phones.

OFFICE MANAGER
Makes sure everyone in the office is taken care of. Handles supplies and payroll.

SCHEDULER
Solely responsible for the schedule of the senator or representative.

CHIEF OF STAFF
Oversees the entire staff.

DEPUTY CHIEF OF STAFF
Helps the chief of staff.

EXECUTIVE ASSISTANT
Assists the senator and chief of staff directly.

COMMUNICATIONS DIRECTOR
Oversees all communications.

PRESS SECRETARY
Engages with the press on behalf of the senator or representative.

SPEECH-WRITER
Writes speeches for the senator.

LEGISLATIVE DIRECTOR
Oversees and helps with policy development.

SENIOR LEGISLATIVE ASSISTANTS

LEGISLATIVE ASSISTANTS
Subject matter experts for developing and understanding policy on housing, energy, education, health care, transportation, and science/technology.

LEGISLATIVE CORRESPONDENT
Drafts letters, tracks legislation, conducts legislative research, and meets with constituents and interest groups.

Senators and representatives spend most of their time in Washington, DC, when Congress is in session. Their teams help them create, write, and discuss policy on behalf of their constituents.

There are also people who help senators and
representatives in their home state or district.

STATE DIRECTOR

Works with the chief of staff and coordinates where the senator goes when they are in their home state.

DISTRICT DIRECTOR

Oversees the senator or representative's office in their home state or district.

DEPUTY DISTRICT DIRECTOR

Help the district director.

STAFF ASSISTANT

DISTRICT REPRESENTATIVE

Serves as the representative for the senator or representative at events and meetings in their home state or district.

These people are responsible for helping, reaching out
to, and understanding the needs of their constituents
on behalf of the senator or representative.

GRANTS COORDINATOR

GRANTS COORDINATOR

Helps constituents, businesses, and universities with federal grants.

LEGISLATIVE COUNSEL

Provides council on understanding legal components of policy and judicial nominations.

CONSTITUENT SERVICE DIRECTOR

CONSTITUENT SERVICE REPRESENTATIVES

Help constituents with problems concerning health care, passports, social security, and immigration.

*Have you ever written a letter to
your senator or representative?*

Now Nima, Peter, and his dad are on the case!

But where could the missing cat be?

Peter, his dad, and Nima walk back down to the second floor.

DID YOU KNOW?
The Capitol has approximately 540 rooms and 850 doorways.

DID YOU KNOW?
There are miles of corridors in the Capitol.

There!

Nima and Peter race down the hall after the cat.

The Rotunda is crowded today! Everyone is here to view the magnificent **dome**. Inside the Rotunda there are lots of paintings, **frescoes**, **sculptures**, and **busts** on display.

DID YOU KNOW?

The Rotunda in the United States Capitol was designed by Charles Bulfinch and completed in 1824. It is located below the Capitol dome and is one of the most popular sections of the Capitol.

They weave through the crowds in **National Statuary Hall**, past the **House Chamber**, and up the West Grand Staircase.

Slow down!

DID YOU KNOW?

Each state can send two statues to display in the Capitol. While National Statuary Hall is too small to include all the statues, you can find the rest displayed in the Capitol Visitor Center.

Looking over the House Chamber from the House Gallery, Peter spots the cat!

DID YOU KNOW?

You can watch Congress in action by sitting in the visitor's gallery above the Senate or House Chamber when Congress is in session.

IN GOD WE TRUST

Hmmm . . . Peter's dad has an idea. He uses his radio to make a call.

Ten minutes later, a woman arrives carrying a tray and meets them downstairs at the entrance to the House Chamber. This is Margo. She runs the kitchen in the **Capitol Cafe**. Margo pulls out a tuna sandwich.

Can you help the cat find its way out?

IN GOD WE TRUST

DID YOU KNOW?

In the United States
House of Representatives,
there are 435 voting members
and 6 nonvoting members, who
represent all the states as well
as Washington, DC, and the
United States territories.

Peter's dad grabs the cat just as the
Capitol Police arrive with animal control.

Peter, his dad, Nima, and Gabriel all head to the Capitol Cafe in the Visitor Center for a snack. Solving mysteries is exhausting. Everyone is hungry. Soon, Gabriel's grandma joins them.

Inside the Capitol Cafe, there are lots of visitors and employees.

Peter orders a tuna sandwich.
Everyone laughs.

After they finish eating, Gabriel and his grandma
wave goodbye to Nima, Peter, and his dad.

Nima's mom is waiting by the **subway** station.

There are three subway systems in the Capitol that connect to the Senate and House offices outside the building. Senators and representatives use the subway to travel between the buildings.

DID YOU KNOW?
The original Capitol subway line was built in 1909.

Have you ever ridden on a subway?

Peter and his dad stop by one of the workshops.

The Capitol has lots of workshops and machinery rooms in the basement. This is where the Architect of the Capitol does carpentry, painting, and facility maintenance work. Peter's dad gathers his things to leave.

We've got one more stop, Peter, then we'll head home.

They arrive at the Capitol Police office. Peter sees the cat! *Can we keep him?* Peter smiles wide.

Search & Find

There are many American flags displayed and worn throughout the Capitol. Can you find and count them all?

Can you find the mysterious cat on each page? What is the cat doing?

There are more than 300 works of art displayed at the Capitol. How many paintings can you find?

Lots of people visited the Capitol today. Can you count them all?

The Real Story Behind the Mysterious Capitol Cat

Known as the Grimalkin, the Capitol cat has been a legend since the Civil War. Union soldiers bunking in the Capitol claimed to have seen a mysterious cat who grew in size and screeched before pouncing. Some have described the cat to be as large as a tiger.

The cat became known as a bad omen as accounts of seeing it occurred prior to significant events in history, including the assassinations of presidents Abraham Lincoln and John F. Kennedy, the attempted assassination of President James A. Garfield, the stock market crash in 1929, the night before the bombing of Pearl Harbor, and on the eve of troops being sent to fight in Vietnam.

Most likely a well-placed shadow on the walls, the legendary cat has gained attention because around six sets of cat paw prints can be found in the concrete just outside the Old Supreme Court Chamber on the first floor of the Capitol. Releasing cats in the Capitol was a common practice during much of the nineteenth century and into the early twentieth century to help control the mice and rat populations. This is most likely the reason for the mysterious paw prints.

Ghost or real cat: What do you believe?

Notable Facts

★ The building of the Capitol began in 1793, with the design by an architect named William Thornton, who was selected by President George Washington himself.

★ In 1793, enslaved people, rented from their owners, played a large role in the building and construction of the Capitol. A commemorative marker is prominently located inside Emancipation Hall in the Capitol Visitor Center to honor and remember the vast contributions made by enslaved workers.

★ The Capitol is an example of neoclassical architecture.

★ The Capitol sits on fifty-eight acres designed by Frederick Law Olmsted, who also designed Central Park in New York City.

★ During the War of 1812, the United States Capitol was burned by British soldiers in August 1814. The building wasn't yet complete, and, although it didn't burn to the ground, there was significant damage.

★ During the Civil War, the Rotunda was briefly used as a hospital.

★ The Capitol is made up of brick clad in sandstone and marble, and the dome is cast iron, weighing 8.9 million pounds!

Sources

United States House of Representatives | www.house.gov
United States Senate | www.senate.gov
U.S. Capitol Visitor Center | www.visitthecapitol.gov
United States Capitol Historical Society | www.uschs.org
Architect of the Capitol | www.aoc.gov
United States Capitol Police | www.uscp.gov

★

Reed, Henry Hope. *The United States Capitol: Its Architecture and Decoration*. New York: Norton, 2005.

Glossary

Architect of the Capitol Originally created as the job of one person, the Architect of the Capitol is now a federal agency responsible for the preservation and maintenance of the United States Capitol Complex, including the Capitol. The title Architect of the Capitol now references both the person and the agency.

Brumidi Corridors A series of five hallways inside the Senate Wing in the United States Capitol decorated by the artist Constantino Brumidi.

Bust A sculpture of a person showing the upper part of their body, from the shoulders to the top of the head.

Capitol Cafe The restaurant inside the U.S. Capitol Visitor Center. It is located on the lower level.

Capitol Police A federal law enforcement agency that protects the United States Congress.

Chief of staff A person who manages, oversees, and advises the staff of a Congress member.

Crypt A large, circular room beneath the United States Capitol Rotunda. It is composed of forty columns to support the weight of the Rotunda and dome above it.

Dome Situated above the Rotunda, the dome of the United States Capitol sits 287 feet high and was constructed between 1856 and 1866.

Fresco A mural painting process where water is mixed with dry pigment and painted directly on wet plaster. The color dries as the surface of the wall or ceiling does.

House Chamber The chamber inside the United States Capitol where the House of Representatives meets to discuss, propose, and vote on policy and legislation.

House of Representatives One of two chambers that make up the legislative branch of the United States government.

Legislative branch One of three branches of the United States government. The legislative branch is composed of the United States Congress, which includes the Senate and House of Representatives.

Mason A person who is skilled in working and building with stone.

Monument A structure created to commemorate an event or person.

National Statuary Hall An exhibition space for the National Statuary collection on the House side of the United States Capitol. Statues are displayed throughout the building and Capitol Visitor Center.

Professional tour guide A person who gives tours to visitors at the United States Capitol.

Sculpture A three-dimensional piece of art. There are hundreds of sculptures inside the United States Capitol.

Senate One of two chambers that make up the legislative branch of the United States government. There are one hundred elected senators, two from each of the fifty states.

Senate Chamber The chamber inside the United States Capitol where the Senate meets to discuss, propose, and vote on laws, ordinances, and motions.

Senate Gallery The upper level of the Senate Chamber where visitors can watch the Senate while in session.

Senate Wing On the north side of the United States Capitol, this wing houses the Senate Chamber, Brumidi Corridors, Small Senate Rotunda, Old Senate Chamber, and Old Supreme Court Chamber. This is also where the infamous cat paw print impressions can be found in the concrete floor.

Senator A member of the United States Senate.

Small Senate Rotunda Designed by Benjamin Henry Latrobe to allow light and air circulation into the corridors of the Senate Wing.

Subway An underground system of transportation.

United States Congress Composed of the House of Representatives and the Senate, the United States Congress is the legislative branch of the United States government.